Bear Country: The Great Frost

A Novel

by Tasia Lawrence

Preface

This book was written based on a dream given to me by the Lord. In my dream, black bears were beginning to outnumber and attack humans. They were walking straight up on their hind legs and using cognitive thinking skills to plan and attack people. I decided to translate my dream into a novel to entertain as well as to encourage readers to take a deeper look at their dreams. The message in your dreams may be signs and or warnings from the Lord. This work is fiction and was written to inspire.

Chapter 1: Sela

"Sela....Sela." The sheer trajectory of my alarm clock traveling from my mahogany wood nightstand into the assortment of fastidiously organized bottles of perfume standing, now shattered on my distressed wood dresser sends Mrs. Tabitha (my next-door neighbor) into a panic. As I climb out of bed and attempt to find my cell, alarm clock or any other time revealing device, I can hear Mrs. Tabitha grasping for air as the heavy tread of her footsteps make their way to my door. "Ms. Sela, everything alright?" she asks while pounding on my door, while simultaneously jiggling my door knob as if the whole lock concept will at some point diminish and she would be granted entry.

I get my bearings and make my way to my front door. I greet Mrs. Tabitha, an older woman with caring eyes, to reassure her of my safety.

"I heard a loud noise and glass breaking. What's happening in there? Are you alright?"

"Yes Mrs. Tabitha everything is fine." I assured her.

"Just one of those dreams again I see?" She asked while glaring into my eyes as if to find the answer there. Having yet to make sense of what just happened I wasn't quite sure what to share with my concerned neighbor. I knew if I didn't give her something she would talk me well into daylight. "Mrs. Tabitha, I am just having some trouble sleeping is all, I'm fine, promise." Mrs. Tabitha begins to walk away, suspicion glaring across her round wrinkled face. "Okay Ms. Sela whatever you say." She says as she walks back to her apartment.

As I walk past the wet, yet fragrant mess left on my now stained wood dresser I check my calendar for a pattern of events. This is the third night this week that I have been jolted from my sleep due to hearing someone call my name. One would assume I was dreaming, but I can almost feel the air from someone's breath on my ear as I hear someone call my name. I begin to scan my modest studio apartment in search of some answers or maybe in hopes of someone I know preparing to emerge from behind my thick purple velvet curtains or from behind my matching velvet papasan chair. It would be my greatest hope to discover that the voice I hear in the early hours of the morning could be an actual person playing a joke (an extremely unfunny one I might add) as oppose to some paranormal occurrence. I check all potential hiding places with anticipation of finding something or someone to help make sense of it all.

I must come to the realization that if the root or reason for these strange occurrences are not discovered I will never have peace, or at least a good night sleep. Feeling somewhat vulnerable in my own place I carefully pick up the pieces to the mess I created and a lay back down.

I see 4:00 am flashing in green on my alarm clock on my dresser. I lay quietly and try not to fall back asleep. No longer able to carry the weight of my eyelids, I drift back into a deep sleep. At 6:00 am I feel my bed begin to vibrate and I nervously ponder the possibilities, then I realize my cell phone is hidden somewhere within my sea of a duvet cover. "Hi Phoebe!" What a relief it was to hear from one of my dearest friends. "Sela! How have you been? Did you hear the news?" She asked with dread in her voice.

"News, What news?" I asked.

"Over 50 people were attacked by black bears over the weekend.

45 people died....and.... Kezia and Michael were two of them.”

“Oh God! Kezia and Michael?” Phoebe and I just attended Michael and Kezia’s wedding a month earlier and they were planning a seven country missions trip with a local outreach organization. The four of us have known each other since high school and in recent years reconnected, which turned out to be a love connection for Michael and Kezia.

“Sela we need to pray. The world needs to pray.”

“Well I’m not much of a prayer, Phoebe.”

“Well you may want to start. During a news clip a member of the National Wildlife Federation said that there has been an increase in breeding among black bears.

They are concerned that there aren’t enough resources to contain them without harming them.”

"Sooo...that means sacrifice human life in an effort to preserve wildlife?" I asked.

"Well....I..um.... I'm not sure what they have planned but we need to be mindful of our surroundings and pray."

Phoebe and I said our goodbyes and I got showered and ready for work. I grabbed an apple and a banana muffin from my refrigerator and head out of the door.

I hop in my hybrid SUV and head down Olympic Boulevard to my clothing design studio in Downtown, Los Angeles.

I turned on the small television in the break area at my studio just in time to hear a news clip about black bear attacks happening around the country.

Oklahoma, Nebraska, and upstate New York had been hit the hardest.

I begin to ponder the possibilities of this issue spreading to California. I mean, the grizzly bear is the state animal for California after all it's only a matter of time before the attacks spread to this State. What would we do? Where would I go? Would there be any point in leaving the state if the issue is spreading across the Country?

If I want to get anything done for the day, I must find a way to clear my mind of this madness and get to work.

I throw on some soothing music and begin preparing my Spring prints for the cutting table. As I hover over the neatly stacked pile of floral print fabric I can't help but wonder if this is the end. The end of the world. Maybe Phoebe is right maybe now would be a good time to pray.

In fear of not being able to cut and prepare my textiles with a steady hand I decide to find a quiet place to sit and ponder. I call Phoebe and she agrees to meet with me for breakfast. I grab my laptop, my apple and muffin, and head over to the outdoor cafe a few doors down from my studio and wait for Phoebe. In the meantime, I order my usual, matcha green tea latte with coconut milk and agave. Phoebe walks over to the perfectly shaded table where I am sitting. Phoebe has always been one of the most caring, perceptive people I know. She can see your tears before they even reach your tear ducts a well up in your eye sockets.

"Sela, you have so much on your mind, I can tell."

"Yeah, I've been having some trouble sleeping, it's kind of strange.... but I probably just need a vacation or something."

Due to Phoebe's intuitive nature, and the look of suspicion on her face is I can tell that I will have some explaining to do, and won't be able to skate over the issue as I would like.

"Strange? How? What happened?" She asks sternly while leaning in closer as to avoid missing a beat.

"Well, I've been having some strange dreams.... well not actually dreams...but...I..I have been hearing someone call my name in the early hours of the morning. I wake up to find no one there." I can feel my palms begin to sweat as this is an extremely uncomfortable topic for me to discuss. I make it my duty to avoid any paranormal or spiritual weirdness at all costs.

"Really?" Phoebe asks with intrigue. "How often does this happen? Have you ever tried answering?"

"Today makes it the third time this week, and answering who? Or what?

You know good and well where I stand with this kind of stuff. It's not my thing, Phoebe!"

"Maybe you should open up your mind a bit. Doesn't seem like this thing (she says with her hands raised while making quotation marks with her fingers) is going anywhere." "You know, there is a story like this one in the Bible." Here we go, I think to myself. "In the book of 1 Samuel chapter 3, Samuel is called out of his sleep three times just like you, Sela! Turns out it was the Lord trying to get his attention."

"Really? Well I don't know the Lord like that for us to be having chit-chats at 3:00 am."

"Neither did Samuel. By the third time he was encouraged by one of his guardians to answer if he heard his name called again and ask the Lord to speak."

Okay, I respond somewhat interested.

"Once Samuel decided to yield to the call he became one of the most respected prophets in history!" Phoebe shared while gleaming with excitement.

Me a prophet, I think to myself....... Nah, couldn't be. Challenging Phoebe, I ask, "So this means I'm a prophet of the Lord now?"

"You could be, or the Lord could have a word for you. You should answer the next time he calls you, maybe it's a word of knowledge." Still not sold on the whole prophet thing, I gave Phoebe a perfunctory nod and sat quietly and finished my breakfast. Phoebe and I embraced, made a mutual promise to meet up again the following week and we went our separate ways.

―――

Three days later. I leave the studio at 11:00 pm after a full day of meetings, endless phone calls and emails, and to top it all off I receive notice that my landlord is selling the building. The stress from having more tasks than time and now having to find another commercial location in the downtown area sends me in a state of complete panic. I log on to my computer and research potential locations for studio space. I find myself distracted by the latest news. Texas, Wisconsin, Minnesota, Connecticut are the latest states to have an increase in black bear sightings. My head began to throb as I begin to succumb to the weight of my stress. I closed my laptop while looking away as to avoid catching a glimpse of headline that I will be compelled to read that will only further compound my problems.

"Sela.... Sela." 3:00 am. I wake up and see my alarm clock flashing green on my dresser where I left it. I hear my name again. I remember Phoebe's words and decide nervously to take a stab at it. maybe If I give it what it wants it'll go away. "Yes...um...who's there. I mean. I am listening. Please go away." I wait patiently for the unknown to appear, respond, or to collect my soul. At 3:30 am I drift into a deep sleep.

Chapter 2: Prognostication

Where are my shoes! I look down at my feet surrounded by twigs and other contents of nature. I look up and around and I am surrounded by trees, bushes and an array of unusual and exotic greenery with splashes of color from the most beautiful flowers I have ever seen. Shades of plum, lilac, fuchsia, royal blue, canary yellow, and seafoam colored flowers nestled sparingly throughout bushes and peeking through the grass from the earth.

A thunderous roar followed by moans sends me into a panic. Noiselessly placing one foot in front of the other I slowly walk, hopefully in the direction opposite the seemingly hungry creature to avoid falling prey. Fear and confusion cause perspiration to seep through every pore on my body. My body is riddled with fear as I can hear treading behind me. I rush to hide behind one of the tall trees. As I lean in onto a bark my hand falls into a couple of grooves. Almost all the trees have markings on them, claw marks perhaps. That's strange! The tallest tree among them stands tall and thick; nearly as wide as a family size sofa and is so tall the top seems to fade into the clouds and is surrounded by light as if to call attention to it. Intrigued, I look around for signs of impending danger and I carefully approach with my hand extended in front of me further than my feet.

As I approach standing inches away from the unusually large tree my reflexes kick in and my hand pulls away. There lie even larger claw markings with fresh rich blood dripping from the grooves. Which way is out! There is not a living soul or creature within my line of sight. I am left feeling that I have been lured here for a meal and I'm the meal. I look down at my white ruffled dress trimmed with lace. I slide my hands down the lower part of my back and rest my hands on my hips. I'm bleeding! There is blood dripping from both sides of my dress. I put my hands in front of my face to see both of my palms covered in blood. I then realize there is blood dripping from the leaves of some of the trees. Sounds of moaning and treading are thick in the air. I gather my bearings and walk briskly through the wooded bush in hopes of finding a trail.

Dimly lit between a row of trees that connect across a path nearly touching the ground, I see a trail. With no other option in sight I make my way through the fence of branches and leaves and with caution step onto the desert sand colored dirt trail. As if I stepped into a parallel world, the sun is shining bright and the grass on either side of the trail is thick and so bright it is almost lime green colored. The trees along the trail hang low and match the unusual shade of green covering the warm earth. Looking back the crowded hole covered with branches and twigs seems to lead to complete darkness. The sun has lowered in position which means it is likely late afternoon and I have been walking for a while and begin to feel anxious about being stuck here during nightfall.

"There are so many of them. How are they breeding so fast?" I am elated at the sound of other human beings. I scurry over to a small house with a porch that seems to wrap around the property completely. My heart nearly skips a beat upon seeing a group of people standing in front of a half-constructed wall of greenery. Three men hastily force a metal fence, at least two feet taller than them, into the dirt as two women jam leaves and twigs between the holes in the tall fence. "It's winter why are the bears up, mom? Dad you told me they sleep all winter." One of the toddlers watching says raising his hands expressing his confusion. "I know baby; they're changing their habits I guess. We're just not sure." One of the women responded with worry glaring across her face.

   "Hello I'm Sela." I announce my presence while cautiously approaching.

"Good Lord! She's covered in blood."

"Where on earth are her shoes!? She's filthy too!"

"Maybe she made contact. But she's still alive." The group talked about me among themselves as if I was not even present.

"Where do you live? Where did you come from? And where are your shoes? An older woman with silver grey hair shaped into a bowl cut asks emphatically.

I look down at my once white dress and my dirty legs and feet and hang my head as I try my hardest to figure out how I reached this place.

"Are you hurt?" I shake my head while simultaneously whispering no.

"Well you better come inside with us. You don't want to be caught out here after dark." I follow the silver haired woman into the house as the children trail behind. The woman points to a door straight to the back of the house and tells me to go get cleaned up.

"There are fresh towels, toiletries and a pair of sweats and socks about your size in the washroom." She nods with a warm smile as I thank her graciously and walk through the beautifully decorated home to the back room. The children run around and past me to another room in the back of the home.

I emerge from the apartment sized washroom and walk down the long hall with several family photo collages placed along the walls accompanied by framed newspaper clippings. The clippings seem to document a sequence of events in chronological order. "Mall attack, 59 killed." I read in a low voice to myself. "Black bears attack again, this time killing 10 at a gas station." Another read. "Beware, they travel in packs." On the wall hang a few more points on the timeline but I figure I've read enough for one day.

"Sela is it?" She pronounced it SAY-LUH but I am in no position to come off as impudent so I let it slide.

"Yes ma'am."

"Call me Persis and have a seat I'll pour you a cup of tea." She turns to me as she pours with a look of curiosity and a bit of confusion asks, "So, Say-luh what brings you to these parts?"

"I was walking through the forest and I..." Before I can finish my sentence, Persis plops the tea kettle on the stove and thrusts her body over to the table at what seems to be lightening-speed.

"And you made it out.... you're alive!" My mouth is forced open due to shock by her hastiness, I shake my head yes.

"Were you attacked? You had blood on your dress."

"It wasn't mine. It came from the trees. it was dripping from the leaves."

Persis pulls her chair closer, inches from my face as if to peer into my soul and see the past through my eyes.

"What else did you see?"

"There were claw marks on the trees. I heard roaring and moaning but didn't see another living soul or creature."

"They're getting closer! Oh Lord! We don't have much time." Persis proclaims, followed by an ominous silence.

"Who's coming? Is someone after you and your family." I ask, curious and afraid.

"The bears! We know when they're close by the marks on the trees. That's how they make their presence known."

Persis stares out of a window in a trance like state and shares the state of events in her town. Black bears are breeding at a rapid pace and have nearly outnumbered humans. They have stopped hibernating except for three days per year during the "heavy frost." The capriciousness of their behavior has made it hard for animal care agencies to protect the public and everyone has been left to their own cognizance. "You know they leave the blood on the trees to taunt us, right Sela?" Persis finally comes to and makes eye contact.

"Bears are not conscious they're instinctive, Persis!" I proclaim, annoyed by her ignorance. "Sometimes we see them huddled in groups conducting…. meetings…plotting our demise. They've gotten smarter. We think they're planning something." I am left feeling lost and helpless as I watch this mature woman transform from matriarchal to detached and bemused.

"Look!" I nearly hop out of my socks from being startled by this clearly emotionally imbalanced woman. Persis points to a field a few hundred feet from the window. It is covered with headstones.

"That's where we have laid them to rest."

"Whom?" I ask while preparing for her next outburst.

"Their victims. the people that were killed this year."

"The bears didn't even try to eat them. They just clawed them to death. Every one of them. The other cemeteries were so full we had to find more space for them." She hangs her head and stares into her lap possibly searching for solace.

"I think you were sent here to help us." A glimpse of hope glares across her face. "Where did you come from? Who sent you? Are you here to lead us to safety?"

I am perplexed and afraid, and have nothing to offer these people. I just want to go home. "I…. I um…I just…" Before I can finish Persis grabs my hand and squeezes endearingly.

"I know God sent you. You can lead us to safety. Have there been any attacks where you live?

"Well…no. Not in my state."

"Tell me Sela, where do we go from here." She asks while gleaming from ear-to-ear.

Chapter 3: Engender

“45 out of 50 states have received reports of black bear sightings and or attacks.” The newscaster shares while wearing a look of complete distress. I tremble while watching the national news clip in hopes this is another elaborate dream I am unaware I am a part of.

“Hey mom. Everything OK in Santa Barbara?”
“Oh, honey pie everything is just fine. You know we have the Lord on our side, right Sela?”
“Yes mom. I know.”
 I answer sincerely for the first time in a long time.
“Mom..um.... I....um...”

"Spit it out Sela! Say what's on your mind." She responds rather impatiently.

"Something has changed. I mean what I'm trying to say is, I've changed."

"What do you mean you've changed? Changed how?"

"I had a dream and I think God wants me to lead His people!"

"Sela! Sela!" She shouted harmoniously. "I knew when I passed that name down to you, Sela "the rock" I knew you were destined to do something great." I can hear mom crying as she cheers me on. Although, I'm not quite sure if they are tears of joy or worry due to what may lie ahead. I didn't have to explain any further mom always had a gift of reading between the lines when the words are too tough to express.

Mom is the true rock of the family. I was named for her.

—

Black bears are the most common species of bear in the world. They are among the shortest of all bear species standing at 4-7 feet tall. Females are known to weigh up to 300 pounds and males up to 600. Their sense of smell is 7 times greater than a dog's and have better eyesight and hearing than humans. Until 2013 there were just over 300,000 black bears in the United States, that number has quadrupled this year. Black bears are near sighted and cubs are born with blue eyes that change to brown within the first year.   Bears have reflective eyes due to a layer of tissue called tapetum lucidum which enhances their night vision.

My nerves get the best of me as I jot down the details of these ferocious creatures on my pretty pink notepad with a pen to match. I gather as much information as possible to prepare for the unknown.

Tryphena, a local Wildlife Association representative stands tall with a bush of ginger curls falling haphazardly from her head and speaks firmly while giving her speech during the press conference. "We here at the Wildlife Association don't want to alarm the public but in order for you to remain protected you all must know the facts." Tryphena says while making direct eye contact with nearly every member in the 200-seat lecture hall. "We chose Los Angeles Academy for Biochemistry to conduct our future conferences and research due to the advanced technology available in their wildlife biology department. LAAB has been gifted with the tools we need to regain control over this growing issue."

I move up a few rows of seats in front of me to get a better look at some of the gadgets Tryphena is demonstrating at the front of the room.

"Wanna come up and assist me with the demonstration?" I hear as I sit down. I look up to see who is being summoned, seemingly involuntarily to the front of the room.

"Hi, I was speaking to you. Do you mind?" She says while looking over her cheetah print framed glasses resting on her heavily freckled cheeks. My introversion causes my heart to pound and my body begins to perspire from nearly every sweat gland in my body. I can feel my shirt begin to dampen as sweat forms in a circle around my arm pits.

"Come on up." Tryphena says with a warm smile while reaching for my hand to help me up onto the stage.

As I plant both feet on the stage and look around at the gadgets in front of me I realize this moment may have been destined. A stitch has been woven into the cloth that will make up my purpose. The inevitability of this moment sends chills through my body and I find myself having to fight my knees from buckling beneath me. I assist Tryphena in wheeling around a large rectangular shaped metal contraption with large holes on both ends. The tall cage stands about a foot higher than my five foot eight-inch frame. Painted over the green camouflage reads Live trap.

"We've noticed more markings on the trees than usual over the past couple of weeks which means we must be prepared for attacks here in California." Tryphena announces while opening the front of the cage to demonstrate its functionality.

Markings on the trees? I have flashbacks of my dream when there were blood soaked claw marks on the trees. I feel my body begin to tremble as I hold on to the cage as I get my bearings. What on earth could God possibly want me to do about this. I scan the crowd of 20-30 something, casually dressed students, entrepreneurs, and volunteers listening intently and sitting still in their shock as Tryphena moves around the table and explains each contraption in detail. I look into their eyes and wonder where they will all be when things go awry. What can they contribute? How many of them will survive?

At the end of the presentation Tryphena and I hand out leaflets labeled "Bear Country: What you need to know to survive." The room falls eerily silent as everyone reads as if their future depends on it, because they all know that it does.

Tryphena approaches me with a subtle yet warm smile and tells me that I would be a great attribute to the Wildlife Association team. She said there was an opening for Research and Control Assistant (her assistant) and the job would entail helping her save humanity, on the West coast that is. I ask Tryphena about the WA's objective. "Isn't the goal of your organization to preserve wildlife?"

"Well yes, of course."

"How can you protect humanity from bears that are clearly outnumbering humans without killing them? I ask somewhat challenging the expert.

"Our objective is clearly changing as we would like to preserve human life as well. We are kind of just figuring things out as we go. Maybe you can help us with that."

"Why me." I ask as I am never one to jump into anything head first. "There is a room full of people here today why was I singled out?"

"Just a gut feeling. I feel like you would be perfect for the job." Tryphena hands me a business card and tells me to keep in to keep in touch.

I walk away and ponder, "why me? What do I have that makes me qualified." I am not even thirty and I've spent the past four years running a design company I don't know anything about wrangling bears. Why would God choose me? Why not a man? Don't they have more upper body strength? Wouldn't one of the strong men in this world be better suited to tackle a bear?

Chapter 4: Transient

Welcome to Hankspaw Nevada is the last thing I see before our jeep curves sharply around a bend of trees. Our driver tries his best to handle the curve and avoid the edge of the precipice which leads to a rock lined creek. Before I close my eyes to avoid witnessing my own death I can feel the jeep lift off the ground and become airborne before slamming into a large bush. We all come to and check on one another and make sure everyone is ok.

The sound of heavy footsteps rushing through the brush of trees and twigs sparks a sense of urgency within us and we try our best to break loose from our seat belts and sit right side up in our overturned vehicle.

The loud, piercing grunts get louder and closer as we begin to panic. Zenas is suddenly pulled from the jeep before she can even scream. Tryphena, Joash and I along with our driver are left frozen with fear. A large hand seemingly painted a greenish brown color reaches through my window and motions for me to exit the vehicle. I hesitantly peek around the shattered window to see a tall man crouched low to the ground covered in a black shag coat with Zenas behind him.

"There's not much time, get out of the vehicle and follow me or you can stay with them."

The man says in a low yet firm tone as he points to a group of bears headed toward the jeep.

We all climb through my window one by one and we are led with haste through a small tunnel a couple of feet away from the jeep. We all bend slightly to avoid coming in contact with branches and twigs that fill the surface of the tunnel. The strange man sprays something inside the tunnel behind us as we enter and motions for us to keep going. We travel a few feet through the discreet bush filled area to higher ground toward a black bungalow with a gated door and gated windows. The man pulls us in before spraying the air just outside the door with the mysterious spray. "Raccoon urine, and anise oil, it masks the scent." The man shares. "That way they'll have a hard time pinpointing our exact location.

We all let out a unanimous "ohhh!" with a sense of relief that the man may not have intended to harm us in any way.

"I'm Uriah." The man introduces himself while taking a moment to scan the group.

"Tryphena." Tryphena offers her hand to greet our hero.

"The Alpha, yes, a pleasure." After a long staring match between the two Uriah shares the current state of his town. Ever since the mass slaying that took place during the annual Fall fair a few months back he hasn't seen a living soul. Most of the residents of Hankspaw were presumable dead or forced to live a reclusive life.

Uriah's countenance began to change as he shared of a warning he received before the attack.

"I would have these dreams, very strange dreams." His head resting in his hand.

"It all started with the killings.

I would see people, lots of people laying on the ground covered in blood, dead.

Over time the dreams would progress and I would see these large figures standing straight up, but not quite human. They would bite and slice people and leave them for dead." Uriah's eyes widened nearly the size of golf balls as he stared at the wall cross from us. The group listens intently, frozen with fear.

"I should have talked about it more maybe people would have left in time and lives would have been spared. I ran out of gas a month ago, and wouldn't make it far on foot. I'm just about out of food and water and the nearest station is over a mile away. If we want to survive we have to go and get supplies."

"The other half of our team should be at the Town Center Theatre in a couple of days. Maybe we should wait there." Tryphena proclaims.

"The Town Center Theatre wouldn't be a bad idea, it is closer, only a half a mile away."
 Uriah says with a glimmer of hope in his eyes.
   Uriah begins shuffling around the room to gather weapons and supplies. We are each given a collection of tools used as makeshift weapons and a small container of drinking water. Uriah leads the way through the long narrow house. He summons Joash to assist him in moving the refrigerator, revealing a large trap door leading to a passage way beneath the home. Uriah motions for us to walk down the steep stairway as he sprays the air and shuts the door. Uriah flicked a switch and one after another, small light bulbs illuminated the entire walkway, which seems to have no end in sight.
"Once we get to the creek a half of a mile up ahead it'll be smooth sailing. The Town Center won't be too far off."
Uriah shares with a hint of nervousness in his eyes.

A glimmer of light shines through the thick layer of hanging vines covered with white leaves. We push through the bush, and without warning we find ourselves wading in water. We unanimously begin to gather our bearings in preparation for the trek. Uriah motions for us to move quietly as he points in the direction of the longest part of the creek. Many of us look down and check our feet, which we can see perfectly through the clear, cool water. We shuffle quietly through the water; the sun fighting to peek through the thick canopy of trees lining the creek. The clear creek is surrounded by rocks. Beyond the rocks lye a thick bed of hydrophytes, with no evidence of dry land in sight.

After a loud and sudden swoosh, Tryphena is suspended in the air by a rope made of thick vined and leaves. The four of us look up in shock as Tryphena dangles from a tree branch, upside down by one of her legs.

"It's a trap! They've set a trap."
Uriah proclaims as he takes a quick scan of the
surrounding area and rushes toward the tree.
"Oh goodness! Who did this? Who would set a
trap here?" Tryphena yells hysterically.
"The bears. Try not to make too much noise we
don't want to draw any attention to ourselves.
Just stay calm I'm coming for ya!" Uriah says.
But it was too late. The bush and trees tremble
due to a sudden rush of a hidden figure headed
in our direction. As the sound draws near we
scurry over to Tryphena to free her from the
trap, only to witness her untimely demise.
Tryphena was ripped from the tree and dragged
through the wet bush before we could reach her.
"It's too late"! Uriah shouts while trying to
prevent Zenas, Joash, and I from reaching our
leader.
"If we follow we will die too! Stay close to the
edge of the creek, near the trees. The traps are
usually towards the middle."

Uriah looks to the South-East end of the creek. Sheer panic on his face. "Hurry! There's not much time!"

The rest of us chose to spare ourselves and continue to face forward. I can feel the blood rushing from my body as I make my way to the edge of the creek. My feet begin to take over as my senses go numb. Uriah grabs our hands, running and panting as the vibrations from the pack of beasts gets heavy on our trail behind us.

"Oh, God please send help!" That was the only thing left to do. The four of us were helpless and we haven't even begun to come to terms with the loss of Tryphena.

Bang, bang, bang, bang, bang! Our reflexes kick in and we duck at the sound of gunshots.

"They're down!' A firm steady voice proclaims. "Over here!" A tall man with dark hair and a stocky build motions for us to walk in his direction.

"They have dozens of traps laid around here. Walk along the rocks." The stranger instructs. "Thanks man! We're on our way to the Town Center. There should be food and water there." The beautiful stranger nods and takes a few extra seconds to peer into my eyes. He shares a look of familiarity before leading the way.

We make our way to the town center and find it completely boarded up. The place looks as though it had been deserted for years. This place is our only hope and shelter for at least a mile so we have no choice but to make our way in.

We notice small objects falling at our feet before realizing someone is trying to get our attention. A petite lady wearing all black waves with delight. The woman motions for us to enter the building through a small door in the ground at the back of the building. The small woman ushers us through the small doorway before slamming it shut and securing it with three wooden security bars.

"Abigail." The woman holds up her finger introducing herself. "Right this way." She says as she points to a dim hallway lit with small Christmas lights laid along the corners of the cement floor.

"We've been here for six months. Thank God, this group of bear experts came by with supplies, shelf stable food and water. I'm certain we would not have survived without it."

"We?" I ask out of curiosity.

"A group of residents from this town. We all made our way here at some point of another looking for shelter after running out of gas and food. Many of us could barely make it out of town due to the road spikes."

"Road spikes?!" We ask in unison.

"Yes, I know it sounds ridiculous but these bears have found a way to set traps like pros." Abigail Shares.

"You think bears set the traps? Not possible! Someone has to be behind all of this."

Zenas protests.

"But what we've just seen happen to your friend seemed impossible. But it happened." Uriah chimes in.

"These creatures have gotten smarter somehow. Maybe they have a heightened level of intelligence, maybe someone is behind this, who knows. What I know for sure is no one has gotten close enough and lived to tell about it." Uriah says.

 "No one except for Matthias, that is." Abigail says, pointing to our hero, who nods humbly. "Matthias goes out regularly looking for people who may have been left behind." She adds.

"Everyone! We've found four more!" Abigail announces our presence to a crowd of people huddled around a bearded man with a small frame.

"Sela! You made it! Where's Tryphena?" Adah, our wildlife travel expert asks with a look of concern.

Uriah, Joash, Zenas and I hang our heads unanimously as we all, secretly hope that someone other than any of us will break the news to Adah. I gently rest my hand on Adah's shoulder and fill her in on the tragedy. I allow myself to fall with Adah as she collapses to the ground in anguish over the news.

Zenas and Joash rush tour aid and bless Adah and I with a warm embrace and shared tears. This was the first moment that we grieved over Tryphena's death.

"We must be alert and prepare. For there will be an opportunity to circumvent our predators. The great frost is at hand. Temperatures will soon fall 50° degrees below normal winter temperatures. Our neighbors in Greenville have predicted the frost will be rapid and the length in time of the drop in temperature is unknown. God is giving us a chance to evacuate this town unharmed. The frost can take place at any time, so for now we must prepare."

"That's Abiathar." Abigail gushes. "He is one of our unofficial leaders. No one knows where he came from and we never get a straight answer when he is asked, but we are sure glad he's here."

"Move the weapons away from the walls. So, when they attack and break through them we will have access to our defense." Abiathar instructs.

"When?!" Someone from within the crown shouts with concern.

"It's only a matter of time. They know we are here. The trees surrounding our dwelling have been marked with blood. They have claimed this territory."

The wise leader couldn't be a day over 35 with a full head and beard of pure white hair. Abiathar shifts his slender frame in his chair to be sure to make eye contact with everyone in the room. He exudes an overwhelming sense of warmth, compassion, and a bit mystery.

"How do we even know if any of this is true!?"

A short dark haired man protests. "No one else heard this mysterious forecast and the radio doesn't even work. Who are you to tell us where to go and what to do? We don't even know who you are. Where did you even come from?" The man says while throwing his hands up in frustration.

"Enough Pharez! He has gotten us this far, hasn't he?!" An older man dressed in an expensive black suit, with a cane to match challenges the angry man.

"No Artemis! We need answers before we move forward. Our lives are at stake here. There are enough of us here we can get out of here now! Or we can stick around here and starve to death, since we are just about out of food."

The room was filled with about 60 people. Many of whom were listening intently to the heated exchange but seemed clueless as to which side to take.

"If we leave now there will be a lower chance of survival." Mathias chimes in. "If we wait for the temperature to drop the cold will slow the bears down, some may even fall into hibernation." He adds.

"Ahem. Excuse me! Actually, bears enter a state of torpor, in which their physiological activities are decreased." Adah shares.

"And?" Pharez asks, allowing his frustration to shine through.

"And they may actually wake up and move around during their winter sleep. Unlike most, usually smaller mammals, bears may wake up, and even eat during torpor. Their short-term hibernation can last weeks or even days. Even if we do act when the temperature drops there is still no guarantee we will make it out unscathed." Adah shares with worry in her eyes.

"We have to have faith. We will not be here much longer.

They will attack before our departure.

We must prepare and stay ready." Abiathar
proclaims.

Chapter 5: The Great Frost

"Everyone with weapons experience come forward. This includes firearms, swords and the like." Abiathar called a meeting in preparation of our mission.

We have been at the Town Hall Center for a few days and the temperature has begun to drop, as predicted.

Nearly every man present along with a few women came forward, prepared to take up arms. Each of the volunteers is entrusted with some form of weapon and a region of the building to stand guard. All the newly appointed watchmen are assigned shifts, as our temporary dwelling must be guarded around the clock.

One evening after a bad rain and hail storm we begin to hear a sequence of knocking sounds along the sides of the building.

"They're checking for hollow points in the walls. That will be their easiest entry point." Abiathar shares while remaining eerily calm. "All watchmen raise a hand." They all comply without hesitation. Everyone without a weapon find a watchman and stand behind them in groups of 3-4.

Our mysterious leader couldn't have possible have known the exact time of our breach in security. Could he?

A loud, aggressive ripping sound fills the room. Suddenly, one of the towns people is dragged through a gaping hole in the wall. As many people that can grab a hold, pull the young man back in to the building. It is a known fact that once someone is dragged away by these creatures they are never to be seen again.

One of the watchmen sticks her spear through the large hole and strikes the bear.

This was enough to shock the animal long enough for us to pull the man back into the building.

The bears begin pounding angrily on all sides of the building. The whole dwelling begins to shake and debris falls from the ceiling.

"It has begun." Abiathar announces with both hands raised in the air, palms facing the ceiling. Many of us watch in disbelief and a few begin to murmur among themselves. "Who is this guy?" Many start to wonder if he is even on our side. There was no time to interview the strange man. The walls begin to cave and some of the towns people fall to their knees in prayer.

We all gather at the center of the room. The watchmen surround us facing what once were the four walls of the building. We are surrounded by a tall rush of smoke from the debris.

"We have to rush the pack. That is our only chance at making it past them. We must rush through with enough force that we can knock a few of them down. Hopefully that will give us enough time to run for it." One of the armor bearers proclaims.

"Forget that, shoot the pack!" Pharez shouts.

"No! we must divide and conquer." Abiathar says. "As soon as the dust clears we split up. Three armor bearers rush to the East, three to the West, three around the corridor leading to the former back door, and lead North West. The remainder of us will make our way around the pack going North East. Once we break up the pack it will cause some confusion and we will have a better angle to attack. Everyone unarmed stay close to your assigned armor bearer.

The dust begins to settle and we can clearly see dozens of beady red eyes glaring at us waiting to get a better look at their next meal.

The group disperses as instructed and a cloud of screams erupt. Panic sets in and most of the people just start running in any direction leading away from the chaos.

And there he stood. Tall and proud, not a worry in the world. Time seemed to have stood still as I watched Abiathar stand smack dab in the middle of the pack of bears. He stood, legs firmly grounded, hands cupped together, unbothered by the chaos. The bears were now facing him, but none of them moved. He was untouchable and unafraid. He glanced over at me and nodded ounce with a sense of peace and security in his face. I knew instinctively that he was letting me know that everything was ok and he was where he needed to be.

Adah grabs my arm, pulling me in her direction. "Sela we need to go!"

Adah and I catch up with the group and we head North. Weapons drawn and ready for what lies ahead, many of us glance behind us to see if our brave leader is still in one piece. The ground rumbles beneath our feet. "Sounds like a stampede." Matthias says as he kneels, placing the palm of his hand on the ground. Before we know it dozens of black bears rush out of the bush before and on either side of us. Once they are within a few feet of us they turn, in a robotic fashion and gallop away. Without missing a beat the pack leaps one by one into large holes in the ground disguised with leaves and twigs.

A sudden rush of cold wing surrounds us like a whirlwind. The sound of cracking, like the sound of glass breaking fills the air. As the sound gets closer we are in disbelief as the ground freezes rapidly before our eyes.

It is the great frost Abiathar spoke of. This thick layer of frost forming beneath and beginning to envelope our feet did not insight panic among us. It was a sign that God was with us and He was giving us time to gather our bearings. It was a second chance at life in this new world where our quality of life was abysmal. All we had to do now was find a safe-haven and hatch a plan to take back our land. All before the Spring Thaw.

www.ingramcontent.com/pod-product-compliance
Lightning Source LLC
Chambersburg PA
CBHW070416120726

47909CB00005B/1671